For Martin,
Lil, Mimi, and
Debbie Pope

Kitten
for a
Day

by Ezra Jack Keats

VIKING

Are you a kitten?

Uh-huh—I think so.

O.K. Follow us!

Lap, lap, lap

Splash!

Lick, lick, lick

Slurp!

Meeeeooooow!

Meee. . .rrruff!

Ooops!

Eeek!

Eeeeek!

Thump!

Sorry!

Puppy,
come home
right now!

Next time
let's all
be puppies!

VIKING
Published by the Penguin Group
Penguin Putnam Books for Young Readers, 345 Hudson Street,
New York, New York 10014, U.S.A.
Penguin Books Ltd, 27 Wrights Lane, London W8 5TZ, England
Penguin Books Australia Ltd, Ringwood, Victoria, Australia
Penguin Books Canada Ltd, 10 Alcorn Avenue, Toronto, Ontario, Canada M4V 3B2
Penguin Books (N.Z.) Ltd, 182-190 Wairau Road, Auckland 10, New Zealand

Penguin Books Ltd, Registered Offices: Harmondsworth, Middlesex, England

First published in 1974 by Four Winds Press, MacMillan Publishing Company.
Published in 2002 by Viking and Puffin Books,
divisions of Penguin Putnam Books for Young Readers.

1 3 5 7 9 10 8 6 4 2

LIBRARY OF CONGRESS CATALOGING-IN-PUBLICATION DATA
Keats, Ezra Jack.
Kitten for a day / by Ezra Jack Keats.
p.   cm.
Summary: A puppy joins a litter of kittens in their fun for a day.
ISBN 0-670-89227-0 (hardcover)—ISBN 0-14-230054-3 (pbk.)
[1. Cats—Fiction. 2. Dogs—Fiction.] I. Title.
PZ7.K2253 Ki 2001
[E]—dc21
2001001613

Printed in Hong Kong
Set in Bembo